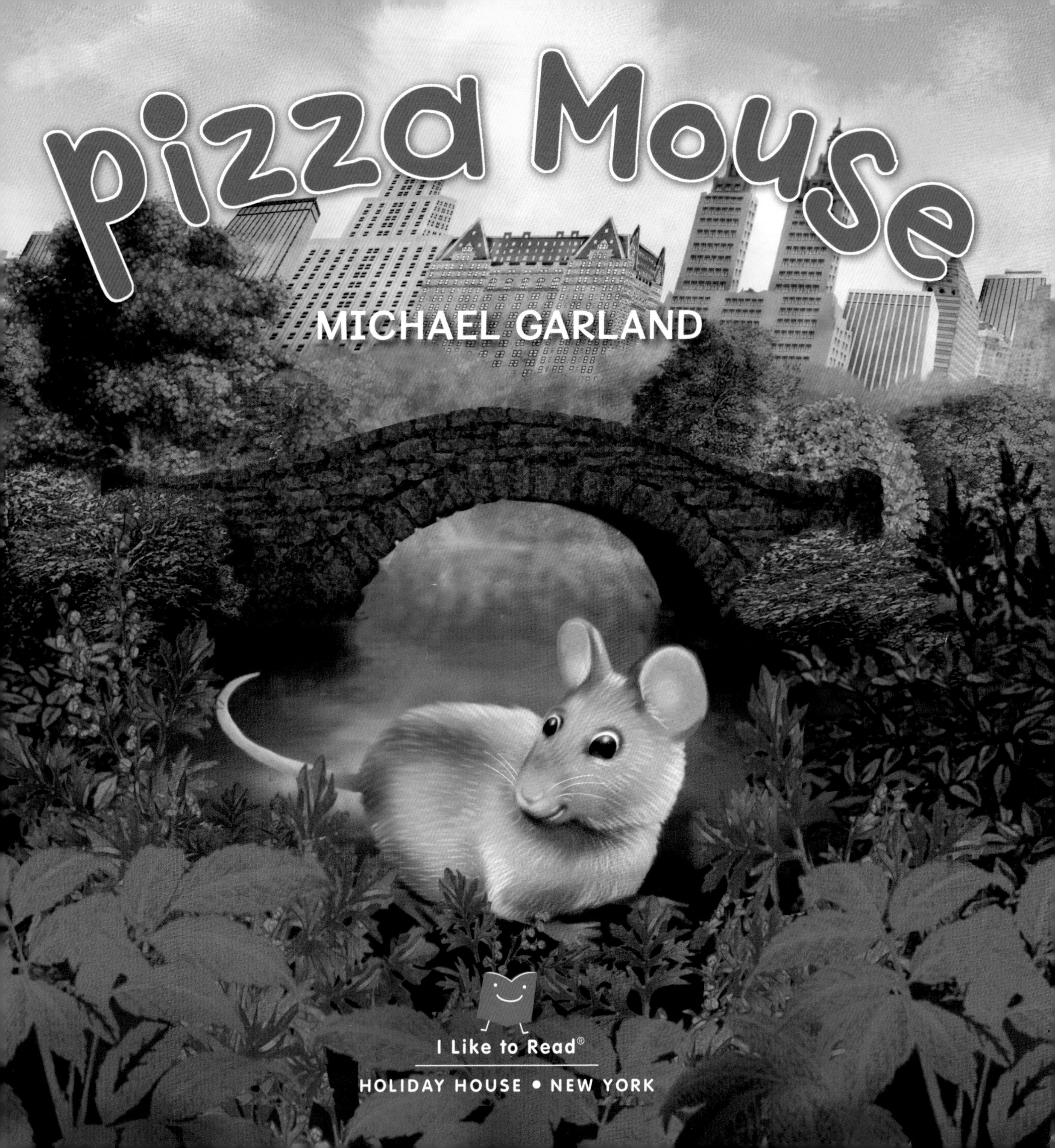

Pizza Mouse

MICHAEL GARLAND

I Like to Read®

HOLIDAY HOUSE • NEW YORK

No one likes mice.

28928
28928
SMITH
MOM

CHICAGO ILL.
AMERICAN
TURTLE

Dogs don't like mice.

Cats don't like mice.

I am a mouse.
So what?

I live in the city.
I look for food.

Thanks for the roll.

I love a big mess.

That Su

Look out for the man!

GOOD
SOUP
Andy's

T
T
123-OH

Look out for cars!

Look out for the bird!

I can hide in the box.

What is in here?

Pizza!

I will take the subway home.

A C B D 1
2
3
4

I take the A train.

Let me out.

Home!

Daddy!